PAPA'S BACKPACK

By

JAMES CHRISTOPHER CARROLL

My Papa is a soldier,
with arms strong and warm.
My Papa is a soldier,
and sometimes soldiers go…

away for a while,
to help for a while,
so I can stay
and play.

But if I could…

I'd ride in Papa's backpack,
and whisper in his ear.
I'd ride with Papa side by side,
so when he goes I'm near.

Mother ~ Father ~ Daug

Me and my Papa,
papa-papa-pa.
Me and my Papa,
papa-papa-pa.

We'd smell the smoke.
We'd hear the growls,
the rumble
and the roar.

We'd feel the sting,
the twisted wind.
We'd taste
the angry rain.

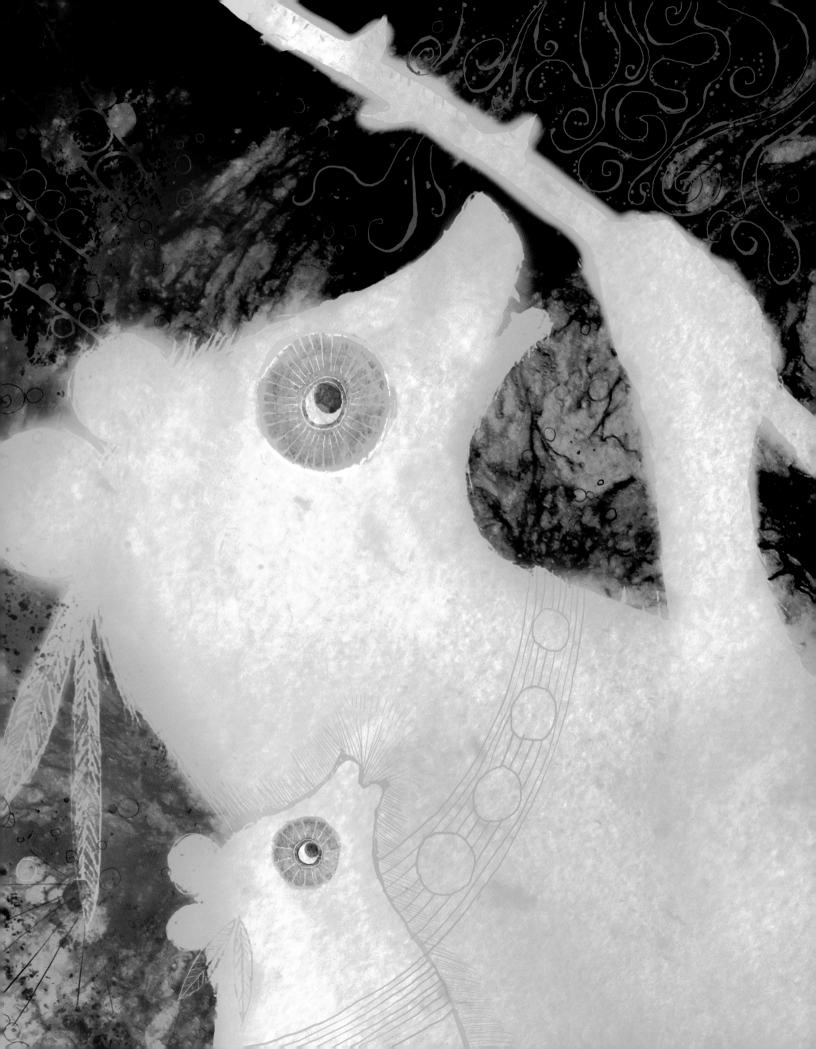

But side by side,
we'd ride the storm.
And side by side,
we'd find our way.

He'd hold my hand.
He'd touch my hair.
He'd kiss my face
and eyes.

Me and my Papa,
papa-papa-pa.
Me and my Papa,
papa-papa-pa.

My Papa is a soldier
with arms strong and warm.
My Papa is a soldier
and sometimes soldiers go…

away for a while,
to help for a while,
so I can stay
and play.

But if I could...

I'd ride in Papa's backpack,
and whisper in his ear.
I'd ride with Papa side by side,
so when he goes I'm near.

To our military families who have surrendered
precious time with their families.

For my sister

—Jim

Sleeping Bear Press

2395 South Huron Parkway, Suite 200
Ann Arbor, MI 48104
www.sleepingbearpress.com

Printed and bound in the United States.

10 9 8 7 6 5 4 3 2 1

Library of Congress Cataloging-in-Publication Data

Carroll, James Christopher, 1960- author, illustrator.
Papa's backpack / by James Christopher Carroll.
pages cm
Summary: Illustrations and rhyming text portray a bear cub who understands
that because Papa is a soldier, he sometimes must go, but imagines what it
would be like to stay near by riding in Papa's backpack.
ISBN 978-1-58536-613-2
[1. Fathers and sons—Fiction. 2. Soldiers—Fiction. 3. Bears—Fiction.]
I. Title.
PZ8.3.C2338Pap 2015
[E]—dc23
2015003425